Abracadabra!

ZAP!
Science Fair Surprise!

Abracadabra!

ZAP!
Science Fair Surprise!

By Peter Lerangis
Illustrated by Jim Talbot

A
LITTLE APPLE
PAPERBACK

SCHOLASTIC INC.

New York   Toronto   London   Auckland   Sydney
Mexico City   New Delhi   Hong Kong   Buenos Aires

For Alex and Zack

ISBN 0-439-38936-4

Copyright © 2002 by Peter Lerangis. All rights reserved. Published by Scholastic Inc. SCHOLASTIC, LITTLE APPLE, and associated logos are trademarks and/or registered trademarks of Scholastic Inc.

12 11 10 9 8 7 6 5 4 3 2 1   2 3 4 5 6 7/0
40

Printed in the U.S.A.
First Scholastic printing, March 2002

Contents

1

Talking Ants, Flying Raisins

"It's okay," Quincy Norton whispered to his left hand. "This won't hurt a bit."

Jessica Frimmel rubbed her eyes. She knew Quincy was different from other fourth graders. He could walk, write, and talk at the same time. He always carried a white cloth napkin in his pocket. He liked prune juice.

But she had never, ever seen him talk to his own hand.

"Quincy, I'm worried about you," she said. She looked at her watch. In only a few minutes, they had to be at school.

"Me, too!" shouted Jessica's little brother, Noah. "Also, me *three*!"

"Ssssh, you'll scare Chuckie." Quincy pulled a jar from his backpack. It was full of ants and leaves. He opened it, turned over his left hand — and an ant fell into the jar.

Quincy held the jar close to his face. "This is Chuckie, my little ant friends. If you all make a nice colony together, I can win the science fair! Thank you, and good luck."

"You're talking to an ant named Chuckie?" Jessica asked.

Quincy frowned. "I guess I should pay attention to Sabrina and Fred, huh?"

"Wow," said Noah. "He can tell the ants apart!"

"No," Quincy said with a smile, lowering his voice. "But *they* think I can!"

Jessica grabbed him by the arm. "Come on, Quincy, we're late!"

Jessica hated being late. In fact, she hated doing anything wrong. Jessica liked things to be Just Right and Just the Way She Wanted Them. Especially on an important day like today. The science teacher was having an assembly about the science fair.

They hurried down Archer Street, turned right on Park — and nearly fell over two boys who were hiding behind a hedge.

"Boo!" one of them yelled.

"Yeeps!" shouted Quincy, nearly dropping his jar.

"Aaagh!" cried Noah.

Jessica didn't jump one bit. It was just the Jones brothers. Their names were Doug and Chester, but they were also called Bug and Pester. Bug was in fourth grade at Rebus Elementary School. He had blond hair that stuck up in the back, and a lip that curled down like he was always sick. Pester was in sixth grade, but he went to a big private school in Rebus called Piggot Academy. He had dark, wavy hair and a big, fat mole on his forehead.

They were snobs, big-time. It was just Jessica's luck they lived on Archer Street.

"Chuckie, the talking ant!" said Pester. "HOO-HOO-HAAA!"

Jessica held her head high and kept walking. "At least the ants have brains," she said.

Noah held his head even higher. "And in school, they'll get even smarter."

"Speaking of ant brains, take Bug with you," said Pester, giving his brother a push. "That way I don't have to walk with him."

Bug tumbled forward. "Hey, no fair!"

But Pester was already heading the other way, toward Piggot.

Jessica felt kind of sorry for Bug. But just a little. "Come on, all of you!" she said. "Bug, too."

Bug curled his lip. He marched ahead, right past Jessica. "I can get there just fine by myself. And my name is *Doug*."

Every year, a mad scientist named Zany Zandor came to Rebus Elementary School. He wore a wild, white wig that looked like someone's old rug. His glasses were so thick you couldn't see his eyes. Stuck to his head was a rubber lightning bolt, and it wobbled as he spoke.

"Good morning, fourth, fifth, and sixth graders!" he called as students came into the auditorium. "Welcome to Day One of the Rebus Science Fair Countdown! Zowie, are we excited!"

"Daaaaad," mumbled a kid named Oliver as he sank into his seat.

Oliver was the son of Zany Zandor, who was also known as Mr. Zandor, the Rebus Elementary School science teacher.

Jessica, Quincy, and their friend and fellow magician Selena Cruz were sitting in the third row, just behind Oliver. Their teacher, Mr. Beamish, was grinning. "I told him to dress up like that," he whispered. "I said it would make the science fair seem more fun!"

"It doesn't," Oliver Zandor whined.

Max Bleeker slid into a seat in the fourth row. He took off his black top hat. Max wore a top hat and cape to school every day.

"MAX THE MAGNIFICENT HAS ARRIVED!" he announced.

Selena stopped brushing her hair for a moment. Selena hardly ever stopped brushing her hair. "Sssssh!" she said, slapping Max's wrist with her brush. "Only one weirdo allowed in the auditorium!"

"Big, *big* news!" Mr. Zandor called out. "This year, I have entered Rebus Elementary in a science fair contest. The winning school will take a special trip to the American Museum of Natural History in New York City."

"Yyyes!" Jessica cried out. "I love that place!"

"Dinosaurs!" shouted Max.

"Gems and precious stones!" squealed Selena.

"A mounted kudu in a realistic African habitat!" said Quincy.

"Huh?" said Andrew Flingus, who was

putting a raisin in his nose. Andrew was the most horrible boy in the fourth grade.

"Now, I know most of you have been working on your science fair projects in class," Mr. Zandor said with a grin. "In two weeks, we will have our first practice in the gym. Everyone can test his or her project. The science fair will be one week later. Just remember — you must do your projects on your own. No help from your parents. No expensive equipment. Just your brains. And that will be enough to win — because we *will* win, right?"

"*Right!*" shouted everyone in the auditorium.

"WE'RE GONNA BEAT —" Max shouted. "Uh . . . who are we gonna beat?"

"I'm glad you asked," said Mr. Zandor, growing very serious. "We will face a very strong school. They have allowed us to use their gym for the contest. It's a school you all know and love — Rebus's very own Piggot Academy."

Max dropped his magic wand. Quincy's pencil flew out of his hand. Selena's hairbrush crashed to the floor.

Jessica could not believe it.

Piggot was the richest school in the state. They had a science lab the size of a football field.

"Those kids are all geniuses," whispered Selena.

"No way," Jessica said. "Pester Jones goes to Piggot."

"Well, okay, they're rich," Selena said. "Same thing."

"I am proud of all the smart students at Rebus Elementary," said Mr. Zandor, looking more nervous than proud. "I know we can do it! We *have* to do it!"

"Look!" cried Andrew. Everyone turned and stared. Andrew pressed one of his nostrils shut and lifted his head high. Then he exhaled through his other nostril — and the raisin shot out. It sailed across the auditorium, landing in Charlene Crump's hair.

"EWWWWW!" shouted Charlene.

"HAR! HAR! HAR! That's *my* science fair project!" said Andrew.

Selena buried her face in her arms. "With him on our team, we are toast."

2

Mystic Max

"ABRACADABRA . . . FLING . . . ZING!" Max waved his magic wand over a model of a World War I airplane in the Abracadabra Club room. "O, MAGIC FRYING MACHINE . . . RISE!"

He stood back excitedly. But the plane just sat there.

"It's *flying* machine, Max," said Selena.

"And you can't make an airplane fly with a magic spell."

"You're right!" Max said. "BECAUSE I FORGOT THE CORRECT WORDS — ZING . . . FLING! There! Did you see that? It moved. I think. Maybe not . . ."

"Enough!" said Jessica. "I hereby call this meeting to order!"

Jessica was the Main Brain of the Abracadabra Club. She ran all the meetings. That meant she had to get everyone's attention — which wasn't always easy.

"You need a gavel," Mr. Beamish told her. "It's like a big wooden hammer. Maybe I have one . . ."

Mr. Beamish was the teacher in charge of the Abracadabra Club. He had a shiny bald head and a pointy beard. He knew a lot about getting kids' attention. He also knew a lot about magic. He was also known as Stanley Beamish, Semi-famous Magician.

Mr. Beamish pulled open his bottom desk drawer. It was filled with hoops, rubber balls, wigs, and cards. "Hmm, no gavel — but try this," he said, handing Jessica a rubber chicken.

Jessica smacked the chicken sharply on the desk. "This meeting of the Abracadabra Club shall begin!"

"Poor chicken," said Max.

"Poor desk," said Mr. Beamish.

"'Jessica opens meeting with chicken . . .'" Quincy said, writing in the Club Meeting Journal.

As the Club Scribe, Quincy wrote everything down. Quincy *always* wrote everything down, even if he didn't have to. He loved writing. He kept four Official Club Books: the Meeting Journal, the Abracadabra Files

(a list of all the club's magic tricks), the Official Mystery Log, and the Clues Book.

"First order of business," Jessica said, "is the science fair!"

Selena made a face. "What does that have to do with magic, Jessica? This is a *magic* club."

"A magic and *mystery* club," Quincy reminded her. "Mystery is our middle name."

"In the olden days," said Mr. Beamish, "science, magic, and mystery were all the same thing. People thought gold could be made from lead. They believed in ghosts and magic spells and creatures who lived on the moon. Really nutty stuff."

"What's so nutty about that?" Max asked.

Max was the Club Numa. No one knew exactly what "Numa" meant, except maybe Mr. Beamish, and he wasn't telling. Most likely it meant "Person Who Everyone Groans At," but Max didn't think so. He thought it meant "Club Wizard."

"I was like Max when I was a kid," said Mr. Beamish with a sigh. "A real Numa. I was never very good at science fairs. I would try to do magic tricks instead."

"Mr. Zandor won't allow that," Selena said. "He's sooooo serious."

"Yes, alas," Mr. Beamish replied.

"He really wants us to win," Max added. "He says we *have* to. It's like the World Series."

"I thought the idea was to have fun and learn," Quincy said.

Mr. Beamish nodded. "Ah, but if our school wins the championship, Mr. Zandor can take credit. And then he may finally get that job he has always wanted — School Science Advisor for the whole state. It's a very important job. He would move to Boston! It's between him and one other teacher."

"No problem," Jessica said. "We'll do something big. Something to blow away Piggot Academy. Something with mystery and excitement!"

Quincy looked up from his notepad. "How do you add mystery and excitement to an ant colony?"

"Or to a flower experiment?" Selena said. "That's my project — growing flowers in different kinds of soil. That's *science*. That's what Mr. Zandor wants."

"Selena, you're the Club Designer," Jessica said. "So *design*. If we can't do magic tricks, let's give our projects a magic *touch*."

Selena thought for a moment. She was in charge of costumes, signs, props, and hairstyles — anything that could make the Abracadabra Club look good.

"Well . . ." Selena said. "I guess a costume or two wouldn't hurt —"

"Signs, too — and lights!" exclaimed Max, flinging his cape. "And MAX THE MAGNIFICENT!"

Jessica grabbed the edge of his cape and held tight. "The word to remember is *science*, Max. No magic tricks. No magic spells. Or we're in big trouble."

"Have no fear!" said Max. "My project — Mystic Transfer — will win the science fair for us. And I mean it."

He walked straight to the sink in the back of the classroom. From the cupboard, he pulled out a plastic cup and a sugar cube. Placing the cup on a table, he grabbed a marker. "This will show the transfer of ink through atmospheric osfusion."

"Through *what*?" asked Selena.

"Watch." Max wrote a large **S** on the

sugar cube. Then he dropped the cube in the empty glass. "Give me your hand."

Selena held out her hand. Max took it and guided it over the top of the glass. "Very slowly, please. Now, because of the moisture in the air and the phase of the moon, we should get a very clean transfer. . . . There!"

He turned Selena's hand over.

In her palm was a big, blue **S**.

3

Feebus from Rebus

"Maaax!" shouted Jessica. "That's a magic trick! That's not science!"

"How did you know?" said Max.

Quincy quickly opened his Abracadabra Files notepad. "'Mystic Transfer . . .'" he said, writing fast. "Tell me how you did that, Max."

"Never — EVER — do anything like that in front of Mr. Zandor," warned Selena.

"He's likely to throw you out of the science fair," Mr. Beamish agreed.

Max sat forward, hands folded. "Okay. I'm serious. From now on, no magic."

"All right," Jessica said. "By tomorrow, let's all decide what projects we're doing."

"Yes," Max replied very seriously.

"I know!" Selena said. "We'll have our own corner of the gym."

"Yes, indeed," Max said.

"Flashing lights," Quincy added.

"Ah, yes," Max replied.

"A big sign," suggested Mr. Beamish.

"A HUGE sign," Jessica said. "With a great slogan."

"Yes, yes!" said Max.

"Max, can't you say anything but *yes*?" Selena demanded. "Don't you have any ideas?"

Max thought for a moment. "What if the sign could float in midair?"

"Maaaaaax . . ." everyone said together.

"Hopeless," said Jessica.

That night, Jessica decided what to make. A volcano.

It was a great idea. Easy, too. First, you made the outside. Then you filled it with water, laundry soap, and white stuff called baking soda. Then you added vinegar and — *splooosh*! Lava came gushing out of the top. Well, not real lava. But it looked real.

In the next two weeks, Jessica worked hard to make her volcano Perfect. She used photos of real volcanoes. She mixed paints to get the right colors. She practiced to get just the right explosion.

By the day of the big practice, she knew

she had it right. She couldn't wait to show it to Mr. Zandor.

That morning, all the science fair kids crowded into the science room. Jessica set her volcano down on a table near Selena and Quincy.

Selena was growing flowers in three different kinds of soil. Pot one was rich topsoil. Pot two was packed dirt. Pot three was salty soil. Pot four was sand.

Quincy's ant colony was set up in a narrow glass container. The ants were just starting to make burrows — and Quincy was busy talking to them: "Now look nice, Chuckie. And Bertha, don't try to lift anything too heavy . . ."

"Where's Max?" asked Selena.

"I don't know," Jessica replied.

Mr. Zandor was heading their way. Jessica quickly poured her vinegar in the volcano. The volcano made a little burping sound. White goo trickled out of the top.

"Good. Keep working on it, Jessica," Mr. Zandor said, moving on to Andrew Flingus.

"He hates it," Jessica said, plopping herself into a chair next to Selena. "It looks fake. And it's too small."

"He said, 'Good,'" Selena reminded her. "'Good' is *good*, Jessica."

Jessica felt something move under her seat. She jumped straight up. "Aaaagh!"

"*I am Feebus . . . the Robot from Rebus . . .*"

A robot, about three feet tall, came rolling out. Wires stuck out on all sides, and a little light blinked and beeped on its head. A crowd of kids was already gathering to watch it.

"*Come to our . . . lovely village . . . for*

the experience of a lifetime. Halfway be-tween here and there . . . on the way to somewhere else . . . the perfect place for quiet fishing, fun people, and that small-town feeling of . . . BLAAT! HONK!"

"Oops!" Oliver Zandor ran after the ro-bot. Oliver's feet were very big, and they made loud flapping noises on the wood floor. He was also very shy, but tall and clumsy, and he nearly knocked over three people.

"Sorry! Sorry! Sorry!" he said, grabbing the robot and turning it off. "Sometimes Fee-bus picks up radio signals. It's the Tuba Mu-sic Hour on WRBS."

"*That* is your science fair project?" Jes-sica said. "A robot who talks about Rebus and plays tuba music? It's great!"

"He should sing or something," said Bug Jones.

Oliver's face was turning red. "Well,

soon the village of Rebus will be three hundred years old. Mayor Kugel says we're going to have a big party for the whole village. I want Feebus to be the star — right, Feebus?"

"*Yes . . . sir . . . Mayor Zandor!*" Feebus said.

"That's kind of a joke," Oliver explained.

Selena was grinning. "We *can't* lose the science fair with that robot on our team!"

"Yeah," agreed Bug. "No one at Piggot is that smart. Not even my brother."

"We won . . . we won . . ." sang Andrew Flingus, dancing around the table.

"Please, children," Mr. Zandor called out. "Go to your own projects now. Very few students have an IQ as high as my son Oliver's. But that just means you should work harder! Oliver, perhaps you can give the other students some help."

"Yes, Father," Oliver said softly.

"DID SOMEONE SAY 'HELP'?" came Max's voice from the science room door. "MAX THE SCIENTIST TO THE RESCUE!"

Jessica ran over to him. "Max, *no*! Not now!"

"This is *science* — just like I promised!" Max whispered. From his cape, he took out a model of a rocket. "BEHOLD, A JOURNEY TO THE MOOSE!"

"He means *moon*," explained Quincy.

Max held the rocket high. With his other hand, he waved his magic wand and chanted, "UP, UP, AND AWAAAAY!"

Slowly, the rocket floated up . . . up . . . up . . . to the ceiling.

Jessica was amazed. "Not bad."

"Thank you, thank you, thank you," Max said, bowing left and right.

POP!

The rocket dropped from the lights. It crashed into Max's top hat and fell to the table — along with little bits of white rubbery stuff.

"There was a helium balloon in there!" shouted Bug. "That's cheating!"

Mr. Zandor held up the balloon and the rocket. "Max Bleeker, are you *trying* to make us lose the contest? Is this your idea of *fun*?"

"I thought it was amusing," Oliver said.

Mr. Zandor frowned at him.

"Helium is a chemical — or whatever," Max said. "And chemicals are science, right?"

"Helium is an *element*," Quincy whispered.

"That's what I meant," Max said quickly. "An elephant!"

"Maaaaax," moaned Jessica.

The veins in Mr. Zandor's neck began to stand out. "I will *not* lose this contest because of some silly magic club. If you do anything like this again, Max Bleeker, I will banish you and every other member of the Abracadabra Club from the science fair!"

4

Distress Rehearsal

"Jessica?" called Mrs. Frimmel from the house.

"Almost ready!" Jessica answered.

She could see her own breath in the garage. She had been up since dawn. Painting and fixing. Making her science fair project better and better.

Today was it. The final dress rehearsal for the science fair.

If anything went wrong — the slightest thing — it was over for the Abracadabra Club. Mr. Zandor had warned them a hundred times that week. "I'd better have an awesome project from each one of you," he had said.

If he wanted awesome, he would get it.

"There," Jessica said, stepping back. "Done."

This time, it was more Perfect than Perfect.

Her little volcano had changed. It looked totally real. And it was huge. Three feet tall. Almost big enough to fit Noah inside.

Forget about Feebus. Forget about Chuckie and the ants. *This* was a science fair project.

Knock. Knock. Knock.

Jessica looked at her watch. Her mom was going to drive her to school in the van. It was the only way to get the volcano there. "Come on in, Mom!"

The door opened slowly. "I'm not your mom," said Bug Jones, poking his goony face into the garage.

"*Get out of here, Bug!*" Jessica shouted, leaping in front of the volcano. "You're spying!"

"No," Bug said, looking at the ground. "My brother told me I had to go to school with you. He didn't want to walk me."

"Well, I'm not walking today," Jessica snapped. "My mom's driving me."

Bug shrugged. His eyes were all moist. "The volcano looks really nice. Can I help you put it in the van?"

Jessica took a deep breath. She felt rotten for being so mean to Bug. After all, he was on her team. "Okay," she said, walking around to the back of the volcano. "But be very careful."

When the final bell rang that day, Jessica nearly screamed with excitement. It was time for the big dress rehearsal!

She was the first to the gym. Her volcano was on a table, smack in the middle. It towered over everything. Selena's project was right next to hers.

Both the girls' projects — and Quincy's and Max's — were covered with beautiful designer sheets. They were thin enough to let in light but thick enough to be mysterious.

Max would not tell anyone what his project was. But this time, he promised, it would be science. No tricks. No helium. Just science.

It was hidden inside a big, blue box, labeled by Max:

Soon, Selena came in, followed by Quincy. "What's that smell?" Quincy asked.

Andrew Flingus was setting up his project at a nearby table. "Come one, come all!" he shouted. "To Fabulous Flingus Fun Food Facts! Learn what happens to food when it rots. *It's a gas!* HAR! HAR! HAR!"

"In your places, everyone!" Mr. Zandor's voice called out. "This is our last chance to see our projects before the big contest!"

Max barged in the room. "Oooh! Oooh! Me first!"

He took out a small key and unlocked his blue box. The sides folded out. Inside was a mess of wires and metal. "AND FOR

MY NEXT TRICK," Max said, "I, MAX, THE MAD SCIENTIST, WILL NEED MY RUSTY MAGIC WAND!"

"*Trusty,*" said Quincy with a groan.

Jessica's heart sank.

"No, Max, not again!" Selena cried out.

Max pulled out a magic wand from his cape. But it was teeny, not much longer than a finger.

"We're dead," Quincy said.

Max placed the wand in a loop made by a metal wire. The wire was attached to a battery with metal rods all around it.

"ABRACADABRA . . . ELECTRO . . . ZZZZZZAP!" Max said, flicking a switch.

The wand began to turn, around and around, on the wire.

Mr. Zandor's frown vanished. The ends of his lips curled up. "Hmm," he said. "An electromagnetic motor. Now *that's* science!"

37

"I don't believe it," said Quincy with relief.

"Me next!" said Jessica. "Come see Mount Frimmel, the Incredible Real Volcano!"

Mr. Zandor was grinning now. "You magicians certainly have changed."

Jessica pulled off the sheet. Carefully, she poured a beaker full of vinegar into the volcano. "Stand back!"

She stepped away and waited. But nothing happened.

Quincy looked over her shoulder. "Maybe you didn't put enough in."

"LEAVE IT TO ME," Max said. "IT JUST NEEDS A GOOD WHACK."

He took out his magic wand and smacked it against the volcano.

With a loud *sproiinnngggg*, a head

popped out — a grinning, shiny jack-in-the-box head!

Greenish goop shot out from the hole, right toward Selena. She tried to duck, but it was too late. *"My hair!"* she screamed.

"Yeeps!" cried Quincy.

"Wow, GREAT project, Jessica!" Max said.

"What is the meaning of this?" Mr. Zandor demanded.

"I — I — I didn't do that!" Jessica said.

Thinking fast, Selena took Mr. Zandor by the arm. "While Jessica fixes that, come see my flower display! Wait till you see the results. You'll *love* this!"

Quickly she pulled off the sheets — and she screamed.

All the flowers had wilted. They hung over the sides of their pots, nearly dead. "Oh," was all Selena could say. "Oh. Oh!"

Mr. Zandor looked ready to explode. He was also scratching his legs like crazy.

"Over here, Mr. Zandor!" shouted Quincy. "Come see Chuckie and the ant colony!"

He took the sheet off his tall glass container.

The lid was gone. The burrows were empty. And the ants were now moving along the floor of the gym.

"ANTS!" Mr. Zandor screamed. He ran from the room, scratching his legs with both hands.

"Father!" Oliver called out. "Can I help?"

"Yes!" Mr. Zandor called over his shoulder. "Tell those Abracadabra kids good-bye. They are out of the contest. OUT!"

5

Hemlock Hill

"Sssh!" Jessica said, ducking behind a bush. "He's coming!"

Quincy, Selena, and Max huddled close to her. Together, they looked through the branches.

It was getting dark. They could tell the dress rehearsal was over, because kids were starting to walk out of the school.

The Abracadabra Club had been kicked

out of the science fair. But they were not going home. Not yet. Not until they figured out what had happened.

Someone had ruined all their projects. Someone who did not want the Abracadabra Club to be in the science fair. Someone who had sneaked into the gym and knew exactly which projects were which — and how to ruin them.

Jessica had a good idea who that someone was.

She nodded as Bug Jones came through the front door of the school. He was one of the last people to leave.

"*Bug?*" asked Quincy. "He would never do something like that. He's not mean enough."

"Or smart enough," added Max.

"I trusted him," Jessica said. "I let him carry my volcano. I told him all about our projects. He knew exactly what to do. And he did it — just so his dumb brother and the rest of those Piggot kids can win!"

Bug walked slowly to the sidewalk, then turned right. The Abracadabra Club waited until he reached the corner of Sunrise Road.

"Now!" whispered Jessica. *"Move!"*

Quietly, they tiptoed across the school lawn. Bug was turning left, the opposite direction from Archer Street.

"He's going toward Hemlock Hill," Quincy said, "to see his brother at Piggot Academy."

"At this hour?" asked Max.

"Maybe Pester had detention," Quincy said.

"Follow him!" Jessica commanded.

"Hemlock Hill is *haunted*!" Selena exclaimed. "No way am I going there. Never,

44

ever in a million years. Not if you tied me up and dragged me."

"Fine, we'll try to solve this mystery without you," Jessica said, starting to walk up the street.

"You will?" Selena said. "Uh, wait up!"

They ran along Sunrise Road, keeping far enough behind Bug. After a while, the road forked around a steep hill. At the base of the hill was a heavy iron gate, covered with vines. Over the entrance, carved in iron, were these words:

Hemlock Hill
Est. 1751
Residents Only
Others Will Be Punished!

"That's not very welcoming," said Quincy.

Bug walked through the gate and disappeared into the darkness.

Jessica followed with Max, Quincy, and Selena close behind.

As they walked up the hill, the air changed. The rest of Rebus smelled like the ocean, but Hemlock Hill smelled of pine trees and chimney fires.

The road grew pitch-dark. The only light came from the distant porches of houses hidden in the woods.

Jessica, Quincy, Max, and Selena's footsteps echoed against the street. The road wound around the hill . . . and wound . . . and wound. Finally, they began to hear noises. Yelling, laughing, *kid* noises.

At the top of the hill, four buildings stood around a grassy field. Two were made of stone and two of brick, but each had a tall, white steeple.

The noises came from a fifth building with brightly lit windows. "That's the gym," Jessica explained. "They call it the Athletic House. There's also a Science and Math House, a History House, a Fine Arts House, and I forget the other one."

"Outhouse, I hope," said Max. "I really have to go to the bathroom."

Jessica led the way across the field. She tiptoed right up to the window of the Athletic House and peeked in.

The Piggot Academy gym was twice the size of Rebus Elementary School's. The walls were lined with seats made of polished wood. The ceiling seemed to go up forever. Across it was hung a bright banner that said, WELCOME TO THE FIRST ANNUAL REBUS SCIENCE FAIR COMPETITION!

When Jessica saw the science fair projects, her jaw nearly dropped to the ground.

Quincy cleaned his glasses to make sure he wasn't seeing things. Selena began speed-brushing her hair, and Max turned as white as a rabbit in a hat.

In the center of the gym was a model of the rain forest ten feet tall and ten feet wide, complete with real falling rain. Near it was a computer slide show about African antelopes, with a screen the size of a person. Not to mention a real car engine sliced in half, with all the parts labeled.

But the most amazing project was a cut-away model of a San Francisco street, showing power lines and subway tracks and about a million other things. Pester Jones was standing next to it. With a flashlight, he was showing Bug all the different parts.

"Oh, my . . ." said Quincy.

"I give up," moaned Selena.

"Amazing," whispered Max. "When did Pester get so smart?"

With the sharp *click* of a switch, the bright gym light went out. The yelling and laughing stopped.

Jessica froze, still staring into the darkened room.

Suddenly, a flashlight beam caught her in the eyes.

"Come out, come out, wherever you are!" shouted Pester.

Jessica tried to duck. But it was too late.

All of Piggot Academy was pointing at the window, laughing at the Abracadabra Club.

6

Spies and a Surprise

"Doing tricks instead of science projects . . . sneaking into Piggot last night . . ." said Mr. McElroy, the Rebus Elementary School principal, walking slowly across his office floor. "This is serious stuff. Mr. Zandor has asked me to officially kick you out of the science fair. And with good reason."

"*Science* was all I wanted," Mr. Zandor said. "And what do I get? Helium balloons.

Jack-in-the-boxes. Dead flowers. *Ants in my pants!*"

Jessica put her arm around Quincy's shoulder. "He didn't do it on purpose."

"None of us did," Selena said.

"I'm sure there is an explanation," Mr. Beamish added.

"I have analyzed the clues," Quincy said. "And I suspect the Piggot kids did it. You see, one of them has a younger brother in this school — Bug Jones. He knew all about our experiments. He would be a logical spy."

"The nerve of those Piggot kids!" Mr. McElroy pounded his fist on his desk. "I will *not* have them picking on our children!"

"But that makes no sense!" Mr. Zandor replied. "The Abracadabra Club was caught spying on *them*! Mr. McElroy, they are interested in hocus-pocus, not science! I won't let them destroy this school's chances to win the science fair!"

"Give them another chance," said Mr. Beamish. "I'll guide them."

"Please?" asked Max.

Jessica looked at Mr. McElroy. Mr. Zandor folded his arms.

Mr. McElroy stared at the floor for a long, long time.

"All right," he said finally. "I will let you be in the contest."

"YIPPEE!" Max cried out.

"But — but —" Mr. Zandor said. His face was getting *very* red.

"Under one condition," Mr. McElroy added, looking Jessica in the eye. "If you find proof that those spoiled Piggot kids ruined your projects, come right to me. Boy, will I give them a piece of my mind!"

"Thanks!" Jessica threw her arms around Mr. McElroy.

Mr. Zandor turned and left the room without saying a word.

All through lunch, Quincy didn't say a word. As he took a sip of his prune juice, he looked left and right. Mr. Snodgrass, the teacher in charge, was busy picking spaghetti out of Andrew Flingus's hair.

"Everyone follow me," Quincy said quickly, folding his cloth napkin. "And be quiet."

"What is it?" Jessica asked.

But Quincy was already halfway across the lunchroom. Jessica and the others silently followed him out the back door.

"I studied the clues again," Quincy whispered.

"It was the Piggot kids," Selena said. "We know that."

Quincy shook his head. "The evidence doesn't add up — even if Bug was a spy. Face it, the Piggot kids were in school all day. Bug would have had to do the damage all by himself. And I don't believe he did. No, I think it was an inside job."

They turned and went through the parking lot. It was packed with cars. At the back, near the basketball court, Quincy stopped near an old gray station wagon.

He pressed his face to the back window. Inside were piles and piles of stuff — electric motors, coils of wire, clay pots, glass tubes, books, videotapes, and computer equipment.

In the middle of it all, near the door, were a pair of scissors, a container of salt, and a big tube of green plastic goop.

Exactly the things that had ruined their science fair projects.

"Who owns this car?" Jessica asked.

Quincy took a long, sad breath. "Mr. Zandor," he said.

7

Piggot

"Mr. Zandor couldn't have done it!" Selena said as the Abracadabra Club raced back to the cafeteria. "He wouldn't ruin his own school's projects. It just doesn't make sense. He wants to win the contest."

"That's why it *does* make sense." Quincy pulled open the back door. "To win, you have to have serious science projects. That means serious science students. He thinks we're not serious. He's worried we'll spoil the science fair with magic. He thinks the Rebus Elementary team will do better without us."

"You think he secretly ruined our projects just so he could kick us out of the science fair?" asked Selena.

"Exactly," said Quincy.

Quietly they slipped back into the lunchroom. Mr. Snodgrass was still busy with Andrew.

"But Mr. Zandor is a grown-up," Max said. "Grown-ups aren't *that* mean!"

Just then Mr. Snodgrass shouted, "ANDREW FLINGUS, IF YOU DO THAT AGAIN I WILL DUMP CREAMED SPINACH ON YOUR HEAD!"

Max shrugged. "Okay, I take that back."

"We all saw the evidence in the car," Quincy reminded Max.

"Yeah, but we saw a lot of other things, too," Jessica said. "A million things. Scissors and salt and different-colored liquids — that's all *normal* stuff for a science teacher. We can't just assume he's guilty."

"Then who did do it?" Selena asked.

Quincy opened up his Clues Book. "I'll work on it. But we better find out soon. Tomorrow we set up our projects at Piggot Academy."

By the end of the next day, Jessica was a nervous wreck. She ran to the gym as soon as the bell rang.

Oliver Zandor was already at the gym door, opening it with a key. "My dad will be a few minutes late," he said. "He's been at a science meeting all day."

The projects had been locked in the gym all day. Mr. Zandor had made sure to cancel all gym classes, saying, "I will allow no one in there to ruin the projects."

Still, Jessica was worried. She wanted everything to be Perfect. She had worked hard to patch up her volcano. Selena had made a new project with other flowers from her garden. Quincy had replaced the ants in his colony.

When the door was finally open, Jessica ran in and checked her volcano. It was fine.

Selena and Quincy rushed in next. "My flowers are okay!" Selena said.

Quincy counted his ants. "Jasper, Ethel, Homer, Margaret . . . everyone's there!"

"MAX THE MAGNIFICENT'S MOTOR IS STILL WORKING!" Max announced.

A truck and a school bus were waiting in the parking lot. A team of teachers quickly loaded the projects onto the truck. Then Mr.

Zandor got behind the steering wheel, Mr. McElroy sat next to him, and Oliver Zandor rode in back to look after the projects. The kids climbed into the school bus — and in minutes, they were all on their way.

"I *told* you Mr. Zandor wasn't the one who ruined everything," Jessica whispered to Quincy. "He had the gym key, but nothing happened to our projects."

"We survived," Quincy said, "but we still have to face Piggot Academy. Their projects are awesome. Our biggest hope to win is Oliver's robot."

As the bus passed through the center of Rebus, the mayor waved at them from the steps of City Hall. "May the best school win!" he shouted.

Soon the bus was climbing Hemlock Hill. The kids became quiet. As they rode through Piggot Academy, their faces were stuck to the windows. In the crisp afternoon sunlight, the buildings cast long shadows across the green.

"This isn't a school," said Erica Landers, "it's a magic kingdom."

The bus pulled up to the Athletic House. As the kids climbed off, the Rebus teachers unloaded the truck. Quickly they began carrying the projects inside.

The gym was full of Piggot kids and their parents. All their projects were covered with sheets. Just inside the door, Pester grinned at Jessica. "Looks like the spying didn't help. Your projects still look stupid."

Before Jessica could answer, a Piggot teacher called out over the speakers: "Greetings, noble scientists of Rebus! All hail to thee!" He had white hair, a big belly, and a bulky sweater with a big P on it. "Tomorrow is our big contest, and we must all sleep like angels. So please set up pell-mell, so we can all go home!"

"He talks weird," whispered Max. "Who's pell-mell?"

"It means *quickly*," said Mr. Beamish.

As the Rebus kids set up their projects, the Piggot kids watched silently. Then, one by one, they started to laugh.

"Is this the kindergarten division?" Pester called out.

"Goo-goo — I go to Webus and I wike science!" yelled one of his friends.

"READY — SET — PIGGOT!" shouted the white-haired teacher.

Whoosh! Whoosh! Whoosh! Pulling off their sheets, the Piggot kids revealed their projects.

"A *rain forest*?" gasped Charlene.

"A *telescope*?" murmured Erica.

"My, my, what fine-looking projects!"

the white-haired teacher called out with a broad smile.

"They'd better be," remarked one of the moms, "after all the work we put in."

"That engine cost me a pretty penny," said a Piggot dad.

Jessica felt herself turning red. The parents had *bought* those projects. No wonder they were so good. "That's cheating," she whispered to Quincy.

"It's not fair," Quincy said.

"Hey, kiddies, show us your best stuff!" Pester called out. "You must have *something*!"

With a whir and a beep, Oliver's robot, Feebus, rolled into the center of the floor. *"I am Feebus . . . the Robot from Rebus . . ."*

"Ahh . . . hrrrumph . . ." said the white-haired teacher. "Well, one of your parents must work in the robot business, eh?"

Oliver smiled and fixed his glasses. "I made him myself. For fun."

Jessica smiled. The contest wasn't lost yet.

"Come on, kids, show 'em what we've got!" said Mr. Beamish. "Ready — set — Rebus!"

Jessica turned to her volcano. But before she could set it up, she heard a splat and a loud *"EEEEWWW!"*

Andrew Flingus was standing over a pile of rotten fruit and vegetables. "Someone put a hole in my Gas-o-meter!"

"My windmill!" shouted Charlene Crump. The sheets of her five-foot-tall windmill had been ripped to shreds.

"Who cut my wires?" someone else shouted.

"The perfect place for quiet fishing, fun people, and — DZZZZIT!" With a sicken-

ing noise, Feebus the robot dropped to the floor.

Jessica couldn't believe her eyes. The Abracadabra Club projects were fine. But one by one, the other Rebus projects were falling apart!

"HEE-HEE-HOO-HA-HA-HA-HA!" screamed the Piggot kids, all hugging and slapping high fives.

Mr. Zandor was turning a deep, deep red.

8

It All Falls Apart

"No contest — you lose! Just *give* us the prize now!" Pester Jones patted Jessica on the head. "Go back to your little magic tricks."

Jessica swatted his hand away. "We'll *never* give up!"

"May I remind you, young man," said Mr. Zandor, putting his face right next to

Pester's, "the contest is tomorrow. *That's* when the judges will come."

The white-haired teacher came running over. His face was pink, and his shirttail hung out of his sweater. "Oh, dear. Oh, dear, dear. This is a sorry mess."

"I demand to know what is going on here!" Mr. McElroy said.

Mr. Zandor took a deep breath. "I must apologize, Mr. McElroy," he said. "You were right to let the Abracadabra Club in the contest. Jessica was correct. Someone is trying to ruin the contest. Someone is trying to ruin *me*. And I will not stand for it!"

"I beg your pardon," said the Piggot teacher. "Are you blaming us for ruining your projects?"

Oliver was holding Feebus like an injured puppy. "It's hopeless, Father," he said sadly. "Let them win. It's only a contest. We could never beat a team like this, anyway." Hanging his head, he walked toward the door.

"Let's get out of here," Jessica whispered to Quincy, Max, and Selena. "Emergency meeting!"

As they ran to a quiet corner, the other Rebus Elementary School kids were madly trying to fix their projects.

"We are toast," Selena said.

"I don't get it," Jessica said. "Mr. Zandor didn't do this — and neither did the Piggot kids. They were *here*. Our projects were ruined before we got here."

"But back in the Rebus gym, everything looked normal!" said Quincy, busily writing in his notepad. "Which means that something must have happened between here and there — in the truck."

"Only Rebus teachers were in the

truck," Jessica said. "Did it stop anywhere? Did anyone else get on?"

"We saw them drive straight from the school to Piggot," said Max. "Right through the center of town, past City Hall, and up Hemlock Hill!"

"City Hall? That's it!" Quincy slammed his book shut. "I know who did it. It was someone we know. Someone we hadn't even thought of."

"Who?" asked Jessica, Selena, and Max.

"First," said Quincy, "I must take a look at your motor, Max . . ."

Moments later, Quincy, Jessica, Max, and Selena left the Athletic House. The sun had started to set, and they could see their breath in the air.

On a ledge at the back of the truck, Oliver was sitting with Feebus. "I knew I shouldn't have tried to make a robot. It was a dumb idea."

Quincy sat next to him. "Hey, don't be so sad. You'll fix Feebus."

"Ahhhh-choo!" sneezed Max.

"Bless you," mumbled Oliver. "It's no use, Quincy. Feebus is history."

"AHHHH-CHOO!" Max wiped his nose with his cape. "Wow, I have to clean out my nose. Do you have a pencil, Oliver?"

"A pencil?" Oliver asked. "Well, yeah . . . in my backpack."

As Oliver took off his backpack and got the pencil, Quincy took Feebus.

"Thanks." Max sniffled, then placed the pencil's eraser into his nose. He kept two fingers by his nostril to keep the eraser steady. Then, slowly, he began to push the pencil up . . . up . . . into his nose! He twisted it a bit, left and right.

Oliver was turning green. "Yuck!"

"Ah, much better!" Max said, pulling out the pencil. He held it out like a magic wand. "Hey, because of my magic nostril, this pencil now has magical powers! Let's see . . . ABRACADABRA — FEEBUS — FREEBUS!"

In Quincy's arms, Feebus lit up. *"Halfway between here and there . . . on the way to somewhere else . . . Rebus . . . the perfect place for quiet fishing . . ."*

"Give me that!" Oliver grabbed Feebus back from Quincy. "He's — he's broken!"

"Not anymore," Quincy said, holding four batteries in his hand. "Not since I replaced these weak batteries."

"But — but —"

Before Oliver could reply, Max and Jessica yanked open the truck's rear door. It was empty inside, except for some pads and ropes.

And scissors. And bits of cut-up cloth. And rotted food. And pieces of wire.

"This is all from the broken science fair projects," Jessica said. "You rode in the back of the truck, didn't you? You destroyed all the projects. Last week, too."

Oliver looked away.

"But why?" Selena asked. "You're the best science kid in the school."

"And my dad is a great science teacher," Oliver said softly. "Good enough to be transferred to some stupid job in Boston."

"But it's a cool job," Max said. "He can boss around all the science teachers in Massachusetts!"

Quincy set Feebus on the ground. *"And here to welcome you,"* the robot chirped, *"is Mayor Oliver Zandor!"*

"That's what you want to be someday, isn't it? Mayor Zandor," Quincy said. "But you can't be the Mayor of Rebus if you don't live here."

Oliver shrugged. "I love Rebus. It's the best."

"So you tried to make us lose the science fair," Jessica said, "to make sure your dad wouldn't get the job. He'd have to stay here — and you wouldn't have to move from Rebus. Right?"

Oliver didn't answer. He was looking over Jessica's shoulder — at his father.

Jessica gasped.

Mr. Zandor walked toward his son. He looked Oliver straight in the eye. He opened his mouth to speak but stopped himself.

Instead, he sat down on the edge of the truck. "I didn't know," he said, putting his arm around his son. "I had no idea."

Oliver looked shocked. "Aren't you mad at me?"

"You bet I am," Mr. Zandor replied. "You owe a lot of kids an apology. Especially the Abracadabra Club."

"Sorry," Oliver mumbled.

"You'll need to tell it to the kids inside. And I have something to tell everybody, too," Mr. Zandor said with a tiny smile. "Now let's go. We have a science fair to win!"

9

The Head of Zandor

"LADIES AND GENTLEMEN!" Max announced through a microphone. "ON BEHALF OF REBUS ELEMENTARY SCHOOL, I, MAX THE MAGNIFICENT, WELCOME YOU TO THE GREAT SCIENCE FAIR CONTEST AT PIGPEN ACADEMY!"

"*Piggot*, not *Pigpen*!" Jessica hissed.

The big day had finally arrived. The gym

was packed with parents, teachers, brothers, and sisters. Piggot students were on one side, Rebus students on the other. Max stood on a small stage under one of the basketball hoops. The science fair judges, two men and two women, waited patiently near the stage.

Mr. Zandor had wanted a big surprise. Something to get things off to a great start. Max the Magnificent had found the perfect idea.

"I WOULD LIKE TO INTRODUCE THE MIND THAT CREATED THIS CON-TEST!" Max went on. "SAD TO SAY, MR. ZANDOR'S BODY WAS TOO TIRED TO MAKE IT TONIGHT — BUT . . . *ABRA-CADABRA . . . BRAINO . . . DRAINO . . .* WE DO HAVE HIS MIND, AND HERE IT IS!"

Max waved his wand. From backstage,

Jessica slowly pushed a four-legged table on wheels. On top of it was a huge, hollow crystal ball.

At center stage, Jessica lifted the crystal ball. Under it was the head of Zany Zandor, the Mad Scientist!

Max winked at Mr. Zandor. Mr. Zandor winked back.

"EEEEK!" shouted one of the students.

"OH!" cried the white-haired Piggot teacher, who jumped so fast his glasses fell off.

"WELCOME TO THE GREATEST SCIENCE FAIR EVER!" Mr. Zandor shouted into the microphone. "AND MAY THE BEST TEAM WIN!"

"Hooray!" shouted the Rebus Elementary side of the gym.

Jessica leaned forward. "You see, Mr. Zandor, magic is fun!"

Mr. Zandor smiled. "This is an optical illusion. And *that*, my dear, is science!"

A curtain closed over the stage. Mr. Beamish helped Mr. Zandor climb out of the trick table. Soft, mysterious music began playing over the gym loudspeakers — and the science fair began.

The judges began on the Rebus side. They walked from table to table, writing on legal pads.

Jessica was nervous as she showed her volcano. But it worked. And so did all the other Rebus projects. Nothing horrible happened. And that was a big relief.

After it was over, Mr. Beamish gave them all a thumbs-up. "Great job, kids! We're doing well!"

Jessica wanted to believe him, but she couldn't.

All the judges were on the other side of

the gym now. The Piggot kids had set up comfy chairs for them. Parents were serving food and drinks. Bug and Pester's dad was using a laser pointer to explain Pester's project. Another mom was giving a speech about her daughter's rain forest. The white-haired teacher was helping explain one kid's home-made computer.

"They are blowing the judges away," Selena said.

Jessica tried to smile. But she knew Selena was right. When the judges finally went to the stage, her heart was pounding.

"We have made a decision," said a tall woman with pulled-back gray hair. "We have seen many amazing projects. But I must say, it was easier than we thought to pick a winner."

"Pig-GOT . . . Pig-GOT . . . Pig-GOT . . ." one kid began to chant.

Pester turned to the Abracadabra Club and grinned.

"One team showed us a full understanding of science," said another judge, taking the microphone. "One team showed us great ideas and hard work . . ."

"I can't watch this," Jessica said. She began to pack up her volcano.

"And that same team showed us something else," the judge went on. "That they could do it on their own. With their own brains, and without help from parents. Our winner is — Rebus Elementary School!"

"Whaaaat?" Quincy said.

Jessica froze.

The judge was looking at them. And smiling.

"She means US!" Max cried, leaping into the air.

He landed on Jessica, who knocked

against the table. With a loud crash, she, he, and the volcano fell to the floor.

"You are *so* childish," Selena said — but she was smiling, too.

Kids mobbed Mr. Zandor as Rebus parents shook his hand.

Bug Jones ran over to the Abracadabra Club. With a big grin, he pointed out the window.

Outside, his brother, Pester, was dragging his San Francisco street to the dumpster.

Mr. Zandor pulled off his mad scientist wig and lifted Oliver off the ground. "We did it, Dad!" Oliver cried.

"You did it," Mr. Zandor said. "You all did. And you taught me something. I wanted to win this badly — for my own reasons. To move on. To get a better job. But this week I realized two things. I realized I already have the best job in the world. And I look forward to winning this again next year, and the year after — and every year in Rebus, Massachusetts!"

"YEE-HAH!" Max cried out.

"The other thing I realized," Mr. Zandor said, "was something the Abracadabra Club taught me — that there is no really good science without a little magic."

"Hear, hear!" shouted Mr. Beamish.

"Where, where?" shouted Max.

Jessica, Quincy, and Selena cracked up. Behind them, the volcano burped.

Or maybe it was Andrew Flingus. It was hard to tell.

The Abracadabra Files by Quincy
Magic Trick #15
Mystic Transfer

Ingredients:
One sugar cube
Water
Magic wand
Black marker

How Max Did It:

1. He wrote Selena's initial, **S**, VERY DARKLY on one side of the sugar cube.
2. He filled the glass with water. Then he stirred the water with his right pointer finger.
3. As he picked up the sugar cube, Max made sure to press his **WET** pointer finger against the **S**. That made the ink from the **S** come off on his finger.
4. Then he told Selena to wave her hand over the glass. But
   a) he held her wrist while she did it, and . . .

b) he PRESSED **HIS POINTER FINGER**
   against her palm.

When Selena turned her hand over, she saw
the **S** that had transferred from Max's finger!

The Abracadabra Files by Quincy
Magic Trick #16
Pencil Up the Nose

Ingredients:
Pencil
Nose

How Max Did It:

**** HE DID <u>NOT</u> PUT
A PENCIL UP HIS NOSE! ****

1. He held the pencil in his right hand. He made sure the back of his hand was facing us — and that his fingers were pointing up.
2. With his left hand, he placed two fingers in front of his nostril. He said he was making the pencil steady. But really, he was hiding the top of the pencil. And the reason for doing that was . . .
3. He didn't really push the pencil upward. He just slid his right hand up the pencil, making it look like he was pushing it. The pencil wasn't moving at all. It was hidden behind his cupped right hand!

The Abracadabra Files by Quincy
Magic Trick #17
The Head of Zandor

Ingredients:
One science teacher (any other human with a head will do)
Magic mirror table

How We Did It:

1. Mr. Beamish let us use his magic table. Under the tabletop, the space is divided in half by a mirror. It goes diagonally across the bottom, from back to front.
2. This means the bottom part is divided into two spaces in the shape of triangles. A person can fit in the back triangle.
3. The mirror reflects the front part of the table. So it LOOKS like the table bottom is totally normal.
4. Mr. Zandor was kneeling in the back section, hiding behind the mirror. All he had to do was stick his head up through a hole in the tabletop!

About the Author

Peter Lerangis is the author of many different kinds of books for many ages, including *Watchers*, an award-winning science-fiction/mystery series; *Antarctica*, a two-book exploration adventure; and several hilarious novels for young readers, including *Spring Fever!*, *Spring Break*, *It Came from the Cafeteria*, and *Attack of the Killer Potatoes*. His recent movie adaptations include *The Sixth Sense* and *El Dorado*. He lives in New York City with his wife, Tina deVaron, and their two sons, Nick and Joe.